ME AND
MY SISTER

ROSE ROBBINS has a master of arts in children's book illustration from the Cambridge School of Art. In 2017, she was a runner-up for Hachette UK's Carmelite Prize, which recognizes innovative work by new artists.

Rose grew up with an autistic brother, an experience that informed and shaped *Me and My Sister*. She serves as an ambassador with Inclusive Minds, an organization that promotes diversity and equality in children's literature, and she has written and drawn extensively about mental health issues. Rose lives in Nottingham, England.

Visit her website at roserobbins.co.uk or follow her on Instagram @roserobbinsillustration.

FOR MY FAMILY

First published in the United States in 2020
by Eerdmans Books for Young Readers,
an imprint of Wm. B. Eerdmans Publishing Co.
Grand Rapids, Michigan

www.eerdmans.com/youngreaders

First published in Great Britain in 2019
by Scallywag Press Ltd, London
Text and illustration copyright © 2019 Rose Robbins

All rights reserved

Manufactured in Malaysia

29 28 27 26 25 24 23 22 21 20   1 2 3 4 5 6 7 8 9

Library of Congress Cataloging-in-Publication Data

Names: Robbins, Rose, author.
Title: Me and my sister / Rose Robbins.
Description: Grand Rapids, Michigan : Eerdmans Books for Young Readers,
   2020. | Audience: Ages 3-7. | Summary: A boy relates how he and his
   autistic sister are alike and different, and some of the ways in which
   they show their love for each other.
Identifiers: LCCN 2019030853 | ISBN 9780802855442 (hardcover)
Subjects: CYAC: Brothers and sisters—Fiction. | Individuality—Fiction. |
   Autism—Fiction.
Classification: LCC PZ7.1.R583 Me 2020 | DDC [E]—dc23
LC record available at https://lccn.loc.gov/2019030853

ME AND MY SISTER

ROSE ROBBINS

EERDMANS BOOKS FOR YOUNG READERS • GRAND RAPIDS, MICHIGAN

ME AND MY SISTER
LIKE DIFFERENT FOOD...

...BUT WE FINISH
AT THE SAME TIME.

MY SISTER LIKES
TO WATCH TV BY HERSELF

SOMETIMES MY SISTER IS RUDE TO NANNA.

BUT NANNA UNDERSTANDS

EVEN IF
I DON'T.

SOMETIMES MY
SISTER JUST NEEDS
TO BE ALONE.

AND SOMETIMES SHE DOESN'T!

ME AND MY SISTER
GO TO DIFFERENT SCHOOLS.

WE DO DIFFERENT THINGS...

...AND WE BOTH LEARN A LOT!

AND MY SISTER DOESN'T.

MY SISTER DOESN'T ALWAYS LIKE HUGS

SO WE HIGH-FIVE INSTEAD!

ME AND MY SISTER

ARE VERY DIFFERENT...

BUT WE
LOVE EACH OTHER
JUST THE SAME.